A Poet's Pen

A POET'S PEN

Reflections on Love, Loss, and Self-Discovery

Merisa Biscette

A POET'S PEN

Copyright © 2024 By Merisa Biscette

All rights reserved. No part of this publication may be reproduced, distributed, or transmitted in any form or by any means, including photocopying, recording, or other electronic or mechanical methods, without the prior written permission of the author, except for the use of brief quotations in a book review.

First Edition, 2024

TABLE OF CONTENTS

*Introduction...**ix***

<u>Autumn: Heartbreak and Pain- 11</u>

1	Haunted by What Never Was	12
2	Goodbye	14
3	I Too Shall	16
4	The Comedy of Broken Trust	18
5	The Tragic Jester	21
6	Man-Boy	24
7	Kingdom	26
8	Once Lost	28
9	Whispers of Shadows	29
10	The Soul's Reflection	32

Winter: Mental Health And Depression- 33

11 Better Days Are Coming **(i)** 34
12 Better Days Are Coming **(ii)** 35
13 Better Days Are Coming **(iii)** 36
14 Better Days Are Coming **(iv)** 37
15 The Deep 38
16 Dawn's Darkest Hours 40
17 Crowned in Fear 43
18 Whispers in The Dark 46
19 A Journey Through Depression 48
20 I'm Lost 50
21 Who am I? 52
22 Out of Place 55

Spring: Healing and Growth- 56

23	Threads of Faith	57
24	Whispers of Farewell	59
25	A Verse of Healing and Growth	63
26	Self-Growth	66
27	From the Ruins	68
28	Lessons in The Ashes	71
29	The First Light	74
30	The Healing of The Rains	77
31	The Quiet Strength	79
32	A Journey Within	83

Summer: Love and Lust- 85

33 The Illusionist's Reign — 86
34 Un-named Maestro — 88
35 A Man with Freckles — 91
36 I Want You — 93
37 Summer Promise's — 95
38 The Ordinary Things — 97
39 Where We Are — 99
40 How I love You — 101
41 Beyond Words — 103
42 A Poem for You — 106

A Poet's Pen — *108*

Introduction

In every breath we take, life cycles through its own seasons. *A Poet's Pen* captures these cycles- each poem a snapshot of the human experience, echoing the rise and fall of emotions, much like nature's own rhythm.

Autumn begins this journey, marked by heartbreak, and lost. It is a season of endings, where love wilts like the falling leaves. The air thickens with the weight of goodbyes, and pain lingers in the space once filled with joy. Yet, within that loss lies the beauty of release- of letting go, even when it aches.

Winter, cold and unforgiving, is the heart of darkness. Here, the poems delve into the depths of depression and mental health struggles, where the mind battles storms unseen. Silence speaks the loudest in these moments of isolation, yet, within that silence, there is a quiet resilience. The snow that blankets the earth is heavy, but beneath it, something waits to bloom.

And bloom it does. Spring arrives as a season of healing and growth. The poetry here is soft, like the first bud breaking through frost-covered ground. It speaks of renewal, of mending what was once shattered, and of the slow, steady rise from the depths. With each new line, hope flickers, reminding us that even the coldest winters cannot last forever.

Then comes Summer- a season of passion and love, where bodies and hearts blaze with warmth. These poems pulse with the vibrancy of life fully embraced, capturing the thrill of deep connection and the joy of shared moments. Summer is a fleeting tapestry of desire and intimacy, a celebration of finding the one who ignites our spirits, leaving us with memories that linger long after the heat has waned.

A Poet's Pen is not simply a collection of seasonal metaphors, but a reflection of the cycles within us all. It is a meditation of the way we rise, fall, break, and heal- again and again. I invite you to turn these pages slowly, to lose yourself in the rhythm of the words, and to find yourself within the shifting seasons.

AUTUMN

Heartbreak and Pain

HAUNTED BY WHAT NEVER WAS

In a trial where I stood as one,

Defeated before the end begins.

In the void where I once felt whole,

Their absence echoes louder than cries,

I am a ghost, a wandering soul.

In a world where truth silently dies,

Their eyes, cold and unrelenting,

Bore into my very soul.

Judgements harsh and unrepenting,

Left me feeling less than whole.

They left unnoticed,

A whisper in the dark,

Their memory, a fading spark

In the downpour of an endless rain,

I drown in what could have been.

What did I do to earn this pain?

What wrong have I, a lonesome tree,

To suffer storms with roots so deep?

To speak with honesty, to see,

Love's river run, then cease to weep.

Their silence, an iron shroud,

Pressed upon my weary chest.

I wander through a clouded crowd,

A lonely bird denied its nest.

They left, a whisper in the wind,

A shadow fading in the light.

I reached, but grasp what might have been,

A phantom in the endless night.

I did no wrong, yet here I dwell,

A lighthouse in a sea of stone,

A solitary, silent hell,

Where truth is met with hearts of bone.

GOODBYE

Though it seemed like a stroll through a sunlit park,

Only the stars knew the shadows that loomed in the dark.

I held your hand, a guiding light from the start,

But somewhere along our path, we drifted apart.

I vowed to guard you, to shelter you from harm,

Yet my promises wandered, lost in my own charm.

In the labyrinth of our journey, I lost sight of your face.

Too wrapped in my own world to chase after grace.

Never did I pause to trace the contours of your pain,

Never did I ponder the storms you faced in the rain.

I walked through our days with blinders on my eyes,

Oblivious to the echo of your silent cries.

Through this journey, I've gleaned a bitter truth,

The sting of betrayal, the erosion of trust.

I can't fathom the depth of sorrow I've sown,

The ache of a love left cold and alone.

When your gaze finally met mine, stripped of its light,

A chill ran through me, a harbinger of the night.

The Spector of "Goodbye" loomed large and grim,

The final curtain falling on what we had within.

In the void of our final parting,

I grasp at the ghost of what could have been,

Haunted by the silence where once we'd been.

So here I stand, at the edge of our story's end,

With a heart heavy and a soul that can't mend.

I TOO, SHALL

If I am your keeper,

Then let it be that you are mine.

If I am your sunshine through each day

Then I shall warm your heart until I fade away

If I am the beauty that you find in the moon's soft glow,

Do you think of me when its light starts to show?

And if I am your friend,

Why would you let this bond come to an end?

But if I am your darkness,

I shall chase away your loneliness.

Though hidden in the night's embrace,

I'll be there, though out of sight, in every space.

If you turn your back on me,

I too shall vanish, like mist upon the sea.

Should you ignore me,

I'll fade like whispers lost in the breeze.

If you forget me,

I shall forget you in kind.

Should you seek to part ways,

Though it may wound my heart,

I will grant you your new start.

Yet, if you come back

Trust that I will no longer be here.

I'll have moved on,

Leaving behind what we once shared,

Our memories gone.

For just as you cast me aside,

I too will walk away,

Forget the stories we wove together,

And let them drift like Autumn leaves gone astray.

THE COMEDY OF BROKEN TRUST

It's peculiar, isn't it, how they wronged you,

And walk away with no weight on their shoulders.

How they play victim in a script they authored,

Acting like the stage is theirs alone, so much bolder.

It's amusing, really, how they still seek your warmth,

As if their betrayal was a fleeting breeze.

They want you to mend their broken façade,

While they shattered the bond with such ease.

It's laughable how they crave your applause,

When their actions were a parade of deceit.

They wore your trust like a worn-out cloak,

And now wonder why you can't just retreat.

It's ironic, how they think you should forget

The transgressions that cut like a knife.

How they expect you to embrace the disrespect,

Like it was nothing but a part of life.

They hope to mend bridges with shallow words,

To revive a connection that was burned.

They seek solace in your forgiveness,

When their empathy was never truly earned.

It's almost comedic how they now tarnish your name,

How they try to diminish your worth with their spite.

They hurl insults like stones in a glass house,

Forgetting their shadows lurk in their own light.

It's fascinating, how they wanted your defeat,

To see you falter and drown in their design.

They dreamed you'd crumble without their embrace,

Yet it's their reflection that shows signs of decline.

It's almost a joke, that after moving past their shame,

They cast you as the villain in a story they contrived.

They hoped you'd suffer, fall from grace,

But it's their own insecurity that's been revived.

And as you walk away, leaving their drama behind,

It's clear they were nothing but a loser in your tale.

You've risen beyond their shallow expectations,

Unscathed, while they fade into their own failed trail.

THE TRAGIC JESTER

It's almost a punchline, the way he flounders,
As if life's stage were his personal joke.
He's a jester in tattered garb,
Clowning with a heart he never truly spoke.

How quaint, the way he demands an encore,
For a performance riddled with deceit.
He plays the fool with practiced ease
While you're left to salvage what's been beat.

It's amusing, really, how he parades his charm,
Though it's a cloak of tattered lies.
He winks and smirks, a master of pretence,
But his act falls flat, a pitiful disguise.

He expects applause for the chaos he caused,

As if his follies were something to admire.

Yet, his script is full of empty lines,

Each act a farce, each word a pyre.

His attempts to belittle your strength are laughable.

As if his spite could dim your flame.

He's a sad shadow, a joke in the crowd,

Who blames you for his own losing game.

It's tragic, how he thinks his missteps are grand,

A pathetic play where he's the star.

But as the curtain falls on his woeful show,

It's clear he's merely a joke from afar.

So, laugh if you must, at this pitiful fool

Who thought he could script your fall.

In the end, he's just a tragic jester,

Lost in the echoes of his own small brawl.

MAN-BOY

There is a face to your name,

There is a soul not even you can tame.

There's some truth to your words,

You carefully chose to spark this flame.

There are consequences to your actions,

You chose to play this game.

There's a boy trapped inside a Man's body.

Hiding behind this wall of fame.

There's a twinkle in your eye

Every time you tell a lie.

There's a conceited boy,

Waiting to be knocked off his high.

There's a smirk in your smile,

And mine, a goodbye.

There's a no return policy

For that egotistic aisle.

KINGDOM

I opened the door to you,

I held it while you walked in.

I made it a safe place for you,

To sell me beautiful dreams.

I built you a fire,

To keep your body warm.

I protected you, from all the storms.

I fed your soul , with love and vanity,

I never knew, you would've left me empty.

But as time went by, you took all you can,

You've damaged my safe place,

From all you've done.

Though I tried to make this place safe again,

You just kept on breaking the barriers,

Down came the pouring rain.

The fire outed, the roof blew away,

The walls came crumbling down,

Still, you tried to stay.

My body shivered from the cold,

There is nothing left in this room of gold.

My heart ached, but my eyes watered down,

I opened the door to you,

But now it's time to take back my crown.

I slowly built this place, piece by piece,

It soon came to mind, it's you I needed to release.

Though you refuse to go, you hid the key,

I broke down the walls, to set you free…

And inside my kingdom,

You shall never again be…

ONCE LOST

Silence isn't as quiet as it seems to be,

Not when your mind is roaming openly free.

Out my mouth, there is not one word,

But in my mind,

There is so much hoping to be heard.

And as the quietness flows around the room,

The awkward emptiness shall finally bloom.

My thoughts of you are no longer meaningful,

Not to a man who's been unfaithful.

As silence carry this weight upon us,

Like the ashes, you drifted into the dust.

So, my mind, it roams with hopes of trust,

But with another,

Of a love once lost…

WHISPER OF SHADOWS

Amidst a forest shrouded in mist,

A girl wandered; courage put to the test.

Sinister whispers and creatures of night,

In the gloomy woods, cast an eerie light.

A strange energy pulsed, lurking below,

Shadows reached, a sinister show.

Eyes closed tight, heart racing in fear,

She shut out the world, what's lurking near.

An echoing voice, familiar and kind,

"Trust in me," it said, a guide to find.

A beacon of hope in the darkness profound,

"Follow my lead, safe pathways I've found."

Yet another voice, deceptive and sly,

Doubt his intensions, "come to me," a lie.

Confusion engulfed her, two paths to embrace,

Both voices beckoned, like a twisted chase.

One voice grew closer, a comforting sound,

Promising sanctuary, on solid ground.

"Don't be afraid," it coaxed, drawing near,

"Open your heart, let me ease your fear."

But the second voice persisted, a chilling breeze

Whispering doubts, causing unease.

"I'd never betray you," it vowed anew,

As dread and suspicion within her grew.

A decision emerged, a battle untold,

To break free from fear's suffocating hold

In the forest's heart, where choices collide,

She sealed her fate in shadows to hide.

THE SOUL'S REFLECTION

In her eyes,

A portal to the depths of her soul,

I witnessed a world burdened by sadness,

Echoing with loneliness,

And etched with the scars of past wounds.

Every glance revealed her hidden pain,

A haunting melody that resonated within me.

She was a masterpiece, a work of art,

Yet, blind to her own beauty,

For all she saw was a shattered heart

In fragmented pieces.

Through those unfiltered, unguarded eyes,

Her raw vulnerability painted a story

Only few could truly understand.

WINTER

Mental Health and Depression

BETTER DAYS ARE COMING

Better Days are Coming

They say,

In whispers that tremble like autumn leaves,

But you've seen so much of pain- the kind the lingers.

Like shadows that never leave at dusk,

Clinging to the edges of every night.

Better Days are Coming

They echo, like a prayer you forgot to say,

But sometimes it feels like this is all for nothing,

A journey through a storm with no end in sight,

No lighthouse,

No warm embrace waiting at the shore.

We never count the hours until it's running out-

Until the clock's hands, relentless as grief,

Strip the light from the day

And leave you alone in the dark.

Time is cruel that way, you see,

A silent thief that robs you blind,

Before you even know what you've lost.

Better Days are Coming

They say,

Though the echoes feel distant,

And love for me became something quieter,

Not a wound, but a thread woven through time,

A subtle shift in the way I see the world,

A reflection in the mirror that has learned to soften its gaze.

You trace the lines of the story,

Fingers brushing the tender places that still ache,

But not from pain- just from remembering.

You wonder if this is how it's meant to be-

If the dawn will finally kiss the horizon,

Where you've been standing all along,

Or if the night is simple a part of the dance

That leads you closer to the light.

Better Days are Coming

You tell yourself,

Though the words feel hollow,

A song sung to many times,

The notes worn thin by sorrow's weight.

And in this quiet reflection, you hold onto the truth-

With all that you are, and all you have yet to become.

You wait,

With hands that have known too much,

And a heart that has weathered the storms,

But still… you wait,

For the better days that are always coming-

But never seem to arrive.

THE DEEP

I rode this wave with hope,

Just hoping to find an island

To call my dear home…

With the current of this deep Pacific Ocean,

The unsettledness of the weather,

I was left with nothing, but a life jacket,

For this storm that I'm under…

As the water level risen into this vicious wave,

Perhaps. I should've ducked,

But the only thing to surviving,

Will be left to float away.

The tumbles, the current from all angles and corners,

Left me breathless and shattered,

In the water made for foreigners.

And as the ruthless, deep slowly calmed,

I rose to the top with a stretch of the palm.

Although my journey is yet to be over,

This deep, I'm not too keen to discover,

For I have felt the raft of this ocean,

And I hope that another doesn't have to go

Through the same emotions.

DAWN'S DARKEST HOUR

Dawn's darkest hour,

I lie awake, trapped between the night and day.

Where sleep is a distant, unreachable dream,

And fear coils around my heart,

Tightening with every breath-

The weight of my thoughts threatens to break me.

Dawn's darkest hour,

Where shame and regret become tangible things.

Heavy chains that drag me back into the depths

Of yesterday.

They choke me slowly,

Their grip relentless,

As they suffocate any hope that tries to rise.

If only you could see beyond these walls I've built,

You'd find the cracks where my soul bleeds,

Where shadows whisper the secrets I've buried,

Where the darkness I hide from the world

Is more real than the smile I force myself to wear.

Inside this fortress of ice,

I am alone, frozen in time,

Trapped with the ghosts of all I've lost.

The voices of my past echo in the silence,

Each one a story of pain I can never tell,

Each one a wound that will never heal.

So, beware of the shadows that dance around me,

For they are born to my deepest fears.

And trust, once shattered, is a broken thing-

A jagged shard that cuts deeper with every

Attempt to mend it.

If you dare to come close,

You will feel the sting of my unspoken torment,

The venom of the traumas I carry within.

And if you find yourself drawn into this abyss,

It's because you believed in the false light of dawn-

But here, in the darkest hour,

That light is just another lie I tell myself,

A flicker of hope that dies as soon as it's born.

CROWNED IN FEAR

In the shadows,

They say, demons find their home,

Not beneath the bed, nor where the dark streets roam.

But deep within, where thoughts take root and grow,

Whispering lies that cut deep and low-

"You're not enough," they murmur, a cruel refrain,

Fanning the flames of an internal pain.

Ex-lovers fade, leaving only the ghost of touch,

Their promises turned to ash; love's illusion crushed.

Friends wear mask, hiding daggers in their smiles,

Eroding trust with every unspoken mile.

Your crown, once gleaming with dreams and light,

Now feels like a burden too heavy to fight.

Time is a thief, slipping through your grasp,

Leaving you trapped in a haunting, endless rasp.

Days bleed into years, an unyielding tide,

While others march forward, you're stuck inside.

Fear aches over you, a shadowy throne,

Holding you captive, making you feel alone.

Moving backward, a dance with the abyss,

Where every step forward is one you miss.

The game is relentless, the wounds never heal,

Blame echoes in your mind, striking steel.

Your thoughts are a vault, locked and cold,

Where hope once flickered, now it grows old.

Hope, once a beacon, now fades away,

Slipping through fingers like the end of day.

You yearn for an end, a release from this night,

But in this crown of fear, there's no respite.

You stand on the edge, where silence drowns sound,

Waiting for darkness, to pull you down.

Yet in the void, where light is unknown,

You find yourself- unseen, yet overthrown.

WHISPER IN THE DARK

In the recesses of your mind, a relentless noise lingers,

Voices whispering "you're not enough," with cold fingers.

"Unworthy, broken"- these echoes steal your peace,

Casting shadows on dreams, never allowing them to cease.

From the innocence of youth to the weight

Of grown-up fears,

You've carried the heavy burden of unspoken tears.

A small seed of doubt, nurtured in silence, it grew,

Into a darkened room where hope feels far and few.

You've shut yourself in, where the light seldom creeps,

Substances your solace in a place where despair sleeps.

The thought of breaking free seems distant,

Shrouded in mist,

Yet there are others waiting for their own chance to persist.

Before you surrender to the storm's unyielding might,

Understand that your pain echoes far beyond the night.

There are hearts that look to you, hoping for your strength,

Even when your own light seems to be at arm's length.

Others, hidden in their own shadows,

Need your light to show,

Hold onto hope, let resilience be what you bestow.

When darkness whispers that ending is the only way,

Remember it's a fleeting shadow, just a temporary fray.

A JOURNEY THROUGH DEPRESSION

Depression, a weight that I cannot bear,

A burden that I cannot seem to share.

A shadow that follows me through the day,

A darkness that won't go away.

It feels like I'm drowning, in a sea of despair,

Grasping for air, but it's just not there.

I'm lost in a maze, with no end in sight,

Trapped in darkness, so deep and so tight.

It's a feeling of hopelessness, which grips me tight,

A struggle that I fight with all my might.

But sometimes, it feels like a losing game,

And all I can do is cry out in pain.

Yet, I know that I am not alone,

That there are people who care,

Who've grown to understand and help me through

To guide me toward a life that's new.

So, I hold onto hope, and I hold onto light,

Knowing that with time, I will find my sight.

That one day the darkness will fade away,

And I will find my way to a brighter day.

I'M LOST

I'm lost, I don't know where to start,

I'm lost, between the mind and the heart.

I'm lost, I can't put it into words or write it down,

They say heavy is the head, that carries a crown.

I'm lost, I feel claustrophobic here,

There's nothing but darkness everywhere.

I'm lost, it feels damped and cold,

It is so silent, yet the voices echo.

I'm lost, trapped in this dark vault,

It's no one's, but my fault.

The temperature is dropping low

And the voices have risen.

The echo, echoes,

Sending me into a deep mental prison.

My screams are of silence,

And my body is weak,

My mind knows the truth,

But still, I don't speak.

My eyes can't shed a tear

But it is filled with fear,

Only my heart knows, what's really there.

My body, it shivers inside this place,

I'd do anything,

to bring back this smile to my face

But I'm lost, and I just want to break free.

Why can't you just let me be me?

WHO AM I ?

Some days,

I am the dust caught in a sunbeam,

Drifting, but not really moving,

Just swirling in circles of light the promises warmth,

But never lands, never settles.

I've become the echo of my own voice,

Faint and distant, bouncing off walls that I built

High and thick to keep the world out,

To keep me safe, but now, these walls are my cage,

And the echo is all I hear.

I am a book with blank pages,

A story that never gets written.

The pen hovers, poised, but the ink won't flow.

It's like the words are trapped in a language

I no longer speak,

Locked away, in some forgotten part of me.

But I love the quiet,

The stillness that wraps around me

Like an old familiar blanket.

Yet, this silence is heavy, a weight that presses me down,

Turning my thoughts to lead.

I am the moon,

Hiding behind clouds,

Afraid to shine too brightly,

Afraid of what the light might show.

So, I dim myself,

Fade into the background,

Where no one sees me,

And I don't have to see them.

There's comfort in this solitude, in being alone,

But it's a comfort that crumbles like sand

Slipping through fingers,

Leaving me grasping at nothing,

Wondering if this is all there is.

I am the withering leaf,

Clinging to the branch,

Frail and brittle,

Hiding the decay with a desperate green,

As the wind whispers what I cannot say…

I am not okay.

But it's easier to stay in the shadows,

To let the day pass without touching it,

To let the night fall without feeling it.

It's easier to be a ghost

That's haunts the corner of my own mind,

Fading,

Fading,

Until I am nothing more

Than a whisper in the dark.

OUT OF PLACE

In a world of uniformity,

I am a puzzle missing its core,

One shape, one space,

But not whole anymore.

A thousand shards,

Each a silent cry,

Lost in the echo of a solitary sigh.

Fractured in one realm,

But scattered in many,

I drift through existence, weary and heavy.

Not belonging, not fitting,

Just yearning to be,

In a world that's too blind to truly see.

SPRING

Growth And Healing

THREAD OF FAITH

In a world painted with fragments of broken trust,

She held onto the delicate threads of faith,

Refusing to let past wounds define her.

Though caution whispered in her ear,

She longed to dance in the symphony

Of genuine connection.

Beneath the layers of scepticism,

Her heart whispered a resounding desire-

To believe, to confide, and to find solace

In the embrace of another.

With every encounter,

She dared to take a leap, defying the odds

And embracing the vulnerability of trust.

For she understood that within

The delicate dance of trust,

Lie the transformative powers of compassion,

Empathy, and the profound beauty

Of shared humanity.

WHISPERS OF FAREWELL

In the depths of my soul,

A poem takes flight.

A sacred truth whispered,

Hidden from sight.

For I've reached a place where indifference lies,

Where love's flame has dimmed,

And a new chapter sighs.

I no longer care about you,

That much is clear,

The love that once blossomed has disappeared.

Though I once loved you,

That much is true,

In this silent space, I bid you adieu.

The memories we shared,

Now fade away,

Lost in the shadows,

Where truth holds sway.

They hold no weight,

For they were build on deceit,

A mirage of love, a lie hard to defeat.

I don't miss you,

Nor the moments we had,

For they were illusions, a mirage that was sad.

In my heart, they crumble, like castles of sand,

As I walk away,

Guided by a stronger hand.

I don't need you,

That truth remains unchanged,

My strength is my own,

My independence untamed.

And although you once held a space within my heart,

From this moment forth, we'll forever be apart.

But still, you exist, with lessons and scars,

A reminder of the battles fought, the wars.

I've grown wiser,

Stronger through the pain,

For in the darkness, resilience I've gained.

I wish you the best, in the kindest of ways,

May happiness grace your every remaining day.

But my care for you has faded,

Like a distant star,

In this poem's sanctuary,

You no longer hold a bar.

I've forgotten you, like you don't exist,

But the lessons you taught will forever persist.

I'll move forward,

Embracing life's brand-new start,

With a heart unburdened, ready to depart.

So let this poem be the closure we need,

A final farewell, as our paths recede.

I release you with love, as I set myself free,

No longer caring for you,

But wishing you harmony.

A VERSE OF HEALING AND GROWTH

In the vault of secrets,

This poem shall rest,

A raw confession, unshared, unexpressed.

For within these lines, I give voice to the pain,

Of a heart wounded deeply, now seeking to gain.

Once upon a time,

Love's fire burned bright,

Igniting our souls with a radiant light.

But time unravelled the threads we once wove,

Leaving behind fragments of shattered love.

In the depths of my being, a storm did brew,

A hurricane of emotions, a tempest so true.

For in your betrayal, my heart was defied,

And the love that once blossomed,

Now withered and died.

With every word spoken, a venomous blade,

Piercing my trust, leaving scars that won't fade.

Oh, the hatred that surged, like a venomous tide,

Engulfing my spirit, where love used to reside.

But in this private verse, I release my disdain,

For hatred, I find, only breeds more pain.

So, I'll strive to heal, to let go of the past,

And reclaim the serenity, I thought wouldn't last.

This poem, my solace, secret decree

A vessel of emotions that only I see.

May it be a reminder to seek forgiveness within,

To mend my own wounds, and let healing begin.

For hatred it heavy, a burden to bear,

While love's liberation lies in the air.

I'll set myself free, from this toxic chain,

And in forgiveness, find solace again.

I'll hold this poem close, for it is mine alone,

A reminder of healing, yet to be fully known.

May it serve as a reminder to rise above,

And embrace the power of self-love.

So, I'll let this poem fade, like ashes in the wind,

As I journey forward, leaving hatred behind,

For in the depths of my soul, love will arise,

And the wounds of my past, I'll learn to revise.

SELF-GROWTH

In the ever-turning pages of my life's book,

I embrace the lessons, every twist and nook.

From love's sweet gaze to friendships shook,

I find my growth, like an open outlook.

Betrayals stung, but I didn't stay,

Through each set back, I forged my own way.

In the realm of self, where insecurities lay,

I learned to be confident, come what may.

In the mirror's reflection, I see the way,

Through self-reflection, I seize the day.

In the journey's rhythm, where doubts may sway,

I find resilience in come what may.

With empathy and respect, I build the bridge,

In the web of connections, we share a ridge.

In the pursuit of growth, as we all pitch,

Kindness blooms, in every stitch.

So, I am a work in progress,

An ever-changing view,

In the tapestry of life, where colours accrue.

Through self-love lens, I find my cue,

To grow and evolve and share that with you.

FROM THE RUINS

There was a time when getting out of bed felt like war,

When every breath was heavy, every step unsure.

I was buried beneath the weight of my own silence,

A garden overgrown with weeds of self-doubt and defiance.

I wanted to reach out, to heal others' scars,

But how do you pour from a cup that's long been ajar?

I was a vessel cracked, spilling more than I could hold,

Trying to light the way for others while my own path was cold.

But somewhere in the stillness, amidst the debris,

I found a seed of hope buried deep inside me.

It wasn't grand or golden, no promise of a perfect cure,

Just a tiny voice saying, "Get up, there's more to endure."

So, I started to plant, not in perfect rows,

But in the messy, tangled places where nothing grows.

Each effort felt small,

Like trying to move a mountain with a sigh,

But inch by inch, I began to touch the sky.

I learned that healing isn't about the grand leap,

It's in the tiny steps, the promises you keep.

It's saying, "I'll try again," when you soul feels numb,

And watering the roots, even when no blossoms come.

I began to see that the ruins weren't the end,

But the beginning of a new story I could mend.

And in helping others, I found pieces of me,

In every hand I held, I became more free.

So, if you're lost, if you feel too broken to stand,

Remember, even the smallest seed can reclaim the land.

Keep planting, keep trying, let your story unfold,

There's beauty in the struggle, in the way we hold.

LESSONS IN THE ASHES

In the quiet aftermath of a tempest's rage,

I've sifted through the ruins of yesterday's stage.

From the echoes of laughter and bitter disdain,

I've learned to see through the shrouds of their feigned disdain.

I've gathered the shards of trust they shattered,

And pieced together the truths that mattered.

In the heartaches' depth and the folly's glare,

I found the strength to rise from despair.

The lessons etched in the ashes of deceit,

Have taught me more than the falsehood they repeat.

Forgiveness comes not from forgetting the past,

But from releasing the grip that shadows cast.

I've learned that their antics were mere distractions,

A carnival of flaws in their misguided actions.

They're relics of a bygone drama I've outgrown,

Characters in a play I've finally over-thrown.

So, here I stand, a spirit reborn,

From the lessons of pain, my heart's newly adorned.

No longer swayed by the jests of fools,

I've shed the old guise, no longer their tool.

Forgiveness, I've discovered, is my gift to myself,

A release from the chains that once caused me to dwell.

Yet, while I've learned to forgive, I'm resolute and clear-

The fools of the past hold no place here.

Their stage is empty, their scripts now obsolete,

I've moved beyond the farce, no longer in defeat.

With lessons learned and the ashes now cold,

I embrace a new chapter, unburdened and bold.

THE FIRST LIGHT

In the cradle of the night, where shadows pressed close,

I lay buried in the weight of my despair,

A seed lost in the earth, cold, forgotten, alone,

Dreaming of a world where the sun might care.

The silence was a scream, yet no voice could break,

A suffocating dark, thick as regret.

The ground above felt like a grave, a mistake,

And I, beneath it, buried, but not yet dead.

I curled in on myself, a prisoner of the night,

Each thought a thorn, each memory a chain.

The soil was heavy with my endless fight,

Against the crushing weight of untold pain.

Hope, was a ghost that danced on the edge,

A whisper of warmth in a world turned cold,

But I clung to the dream, to the fragile pledge,

That somewhere beyond, the sun is still bold.

The night held me tight in it's cruel embrace,

Every breath a battle, every heartbeat a plea,

But then a crack appeared, a trembling trace,

Of light that promised, "you will be free."

The earth around me, soaked in tears,

Began to break as my roots sought release.

The first light touched me, soft on my fears,

And the darkness trembled, began to cease.

For I was a seed, once lost, now found,

In the coldest soil, where no light had shone,

The first light reached down, without a sound,

And I knew, somehow, I was not alone.

But the sadness lingered, in every ray,

A reminder of the night I spent in chains.

Each beam of light both a comfort and dismay,

For the scars remained, the ghostly stains.

Still, I rose from the depths, from the suffocating night,

With the first light guiding, pulling me from grief,

I shed my husk, though it clung with might,

And stepped into the world, though it felt like a thief.

The first light danced, yet, tears streaked my leaves,

For the darkness had marked me, made me cold.

I rose, but with a sorrow that never leaves,

A reminder that even the strong can fold.

THE HEALING OF RAINS

Once, I feared the rain, as if it were a storm
That threatened to unravel the solace I'd formed.
Its drops, like whispers of shadows and strife,
Fell heavy, a curtain on the edges of life.

I stood under skies that wept with sorrow's grace,
Seeking shelter from tears that might touch my face.
But as the storm raged and darkness unfurled,
I learned that the rain could mend a broken world.

Each drop was a mirror of my hidden pain,
A reflection of struggles, a way to explain.
In its cool touch, I felt the old wounds start to fade,
As the rain worked its magic, my fears began to evade.

The earth embraced the rain with roots deep and wise,
And I too, found solace in the storm's gentle guise.
What I once saw as a tempest of fears and despair,
Transformed into a balm, a tender repair.

The rain taught me that growth could come from the storm,
That beneath the heavy clouds, life could transform.
Its whispers, once daunting, now a soothing refrain,
Guided me gently through the trials and pain.

Now, I stand in the aftermath, where the light gently sways,
Grateful for the rain that paved these brighter days.
For what was once feared, now nurtures, and sustains,
In the healing rain's embrace, I shed my old chains.

And so, the storm that once shadowed my soul
Has become the rain that helps me feel whole.
In its quiet grace, I found my own rebirth,
A testament to the rain's profound worth.

THE QUIET STRENGTH

In the shadow of the towering pines,

Where sunlight barely touches, barely finds.

A seed was sown in a bed of cold earth,

A tiny spark, hidden, unsure of its worth.

It found itself in the silence of night,

No warmth, no guiding light in sight.

The ground was hard, unyielding, and tight,

But it clung to life with all its might.

Below the surface, where darkness reigns,

It grew, tangled in a web of unseen chains.

It drank from sorrows buried deep,

Fed on tears no one dared to weep.

The storms above, they screamed and howled,

But the roots below, they stood defiled.

Each drop of rain, each blast of wind,

Was a battle lost, a battle pinned.

Yet, deep in the soil, it found its way,

In the darkest night, it learned to stay.

It wrapped around rocks, embracing the clay,

It fought to live another day.

With every crack in the earth,

Every tear in the bark,

It whispered strength in the deepest dark.

For in the quiet, where no one sees,

It grew stronger beneath the trees.

Winter came with its biting frost,

But the roots below counted not the cost.

They held on tight, they would not break,

For something deeper was at stake.

Each scar, each unseen wound,

Was where it fought, where it was hewn.

For in the silence, in the darkest place,

It found its strength, its saving grace.

Now, when spring breathes life above,

It's the roots that whisper of battles won.

The leaves may reach for the sky,

But it's the roots that never say die.

So, here I stand, unseen scars and all,

A testament to the falls, to every crawl.

For the quiet strength that holds me near,

Is built on every single tear.

The world may only see the tree,

But below, the roots are the key.

In every struggle, in every fight,

The roots held on, out of sight.

I am those roots, deep and true,

In every darkness, I pull through.

The world may shake, the world may quake,

But these roots, they will never break.

In the stillness, in the silent night,

Is where I learned to fight.

For the quiet strength that grows below,

Is where I learned to never let go.

A JOURNEY WITHIN

In the vast realm of existence's grand design,

A poem emerges, to impart lessons divine.

As we journey through life's intricate terrain,

Let wisdom's gentle touch be our constant reign.

Embrace the lessons gifted along our way,

For growth blooms from experiences, day by day.

In every challenge lies an opportunity to learn,

To shape our character, to discern and discern.

Let ambition ignite, like a fervent flame,

Dream boldly, set sail with unwavering aim.

But remember, true success is not just wealth or fame,

It lies in purpose, in a heart set aflame.

Respect, a foundation for harmonious ties,

Honouring others, seeing through empathetic eyes.

Embrace diverse voices, let compassion lead,

For in unity and understanding, we plant love's seed.

Confidence, dear soul, let it radiate from within,

A beacon of self-belief, a dance you gracefully spin.

Embrace your strengths, for they are truly profound,

And nurture your spirit, let self-doubt be unwound.

When missteps occur, be apologetic and sincere,

With humility, mend what might have caused a tear.

For growth lies not just in our triumphs bold,

But in how we rise when our apologies are told.

SUMMER

LOVE AND LUST

THE ILLUSIONIST'S REIGN

In a realm of delusion,

A man sought his throne,

Yearning to be worshipped, to claim his own.

But in his heart's depths, a void was sown,

Craving validation, his true self unknown.

He demanded reverence, to be treated like gold,

While denying others the respect they were owed.

Boosting himself up, his ego uncontrolled,

Yet, deep down, seeking approval untold.

He'd put on a show, with his boys in tow,

Seeking admiration, the spotlight aglow.

But lost in his fantasies, the truth began to show,

A man drowning in insecurities, refusing to let go.

He craved control, yet, recoiled at the same,

Wanting dominance but resisting the game.

Speaking over others, with arrogance aflame,

Yet, hating when his voice was challenged, tamed.

He saw himself as a prize, above the rest,

Yet, beneath the façade, a coward's unrest.

Begging for attention, his soul's desperate quest,

Yearning to be chosen, though he failed the test.

In his misguided pursuit, he failed to see,

That true worth isn't in begging, nor decree.

For better men existed, far wiser and free,

Seeing through his charade, his true self they'd see.

So, the man who demanded allegiance and more,

Found himself longing for what lay beyond his door.

In his plea for love, his desperation wore,

As the truth prevailed, he was nothing to adore.

UNNAMED MAESTRO

In a world where words weave their spells,

There dwells a man, a charm that compels.

With wit and grace, he graces the scene,

A tantalising enigma, this charming machine

His eyes, like stars, twinkle with delight,

As he spins his tales, casting spells in the night.

His lips, a dance of silver and gold,

Charisma dripping from every word he has told.

No name he carries, this enigmatic man,

A mystery wrapped in a dashing tan.

His mind, a treasure trove of endless thought,

A wellspring of knowledge that cannot be bought.

In the halls of wisdom, he is adored,

His intellect celebrated; his presence adored.

He speaks with eloquence, his words refined,

Captivating minds, leaving no soul behind.

A master of persuasion, his tongue never falters,

Turning adversaries into allies, dividing their alters.

He navigates through life, his path never ruffled,

A puzzle for many, his secrets remain muffled.

He loves, but not the love that you may seek,

For his heart already belongs to a love that's unique.

He has a passion for life, for knowledge, and more,

A burning desire that can never be ignored.

Through city streets, he weaves his way,

A symphony of footsteps, the rhythm at play.

He walks with purpose, his charm a steady breeze,

Leaving behind whispers and hearts at ease.

In every room he enters, attention he commands,

A charismatic maestro, orchestrating grandstands.

Yet, beneath his allure, a humble heart does beat,

A genuine spirit, no trace of deceit.

Oh, how he enchants with his captivating ways,

Unveiling a world filled with wonder and praise.

This intelligent, handsome, mysterious being,

A tapestry of enigma, forever intriguing.

A MAN WITH FRECKLES

A man with freckles, a work of art,
Each little speckle, a piece of heart.
On his skin, they dance and play,
A symphony of beauty, day by day.
His eyes twinkle, he has a smile so bright,
With freckles on his cheeks, what a sight!
His skin kissed by the sun, oh so fine,
A masterpiece of nature, so divine.
Each freckle tells a story, a tale to share,
Of laughter, of love, and moments rare.
They paint a picture of a life well-lived,
A man with freckles, so sweet and vivid.

And though some may see them as mere spots,

To me, they are a canvas, with no dots.

A man with freckles, a work of art,

A beautiful creation, from end to start.

I WANT YOU

I want your breath tracing my skin,

Your touch igniting every corner of my craving,

Your fingers, mapping out the contours of my hidden longings.

I crave your lips,

Grazing my most intimate thoughts,

Brushed on fevered skin,

Traces the path, where sins begin.

Eyes locked, we lose all sense of time,

In the curve of your lips, I taste the crime.

A kiss that lingers, so soft and deep,

In the heat of the night, we're lost, we're steep.

You trace my curves with hungry eyes,

A fiery gaze that never lies.

Your breath is a promise, hot and deep,

In the silence where our fantasies creep.

My skin tingles beneath your hands,

Exploring terrains of forbidden lands.

You rod exploring the intricate patterns of my pleasure,

With a depth beyond mere measure.

Our bodies spinning stories in the darkened bed,

Where whispered moans and fevered sighs are softly said.

With every thrust, kiss, touch, you'll find,

I can't get enough of you,

My body, my heart, and my mind.

SUMMER PROMISES

In summer's light,

Where the days stetch long,

I find myself where I truly belong.

His touch, a gentle reminder of trust,

In the small acts, our love's core is thrust.

Perhaps I'm lucky in this fleeting span,

To share a life with a caring man.

He holds the door, not for praise, but love,

A simple gesture, like a gift from above.

We speak in whispers under moonlit skies,

Where the warmth of his hand meets my tired eyes.

His words are true, no grandiose claim,

Just quiet assurance that ease the pain.

For I am proud, more than words can say,

Of the man you are in each passing day.

It's not in the grand or the ostentatious flair,

But in your constant care, I find love rare.

THE ORDINARY THINGS

We don't need grand gestures,

or sweeping declarations-

Just the quiet hum of the morning,

The way your hand finds mine while we brew coffee,

Our small rituals that hold us close.

In the shuffle of the kitchen,

Where I read you my latest poem

And you offer gentle advice,

I find the real love-

Not in the big moments, but in the everyday,

Where our lives overlap in the softest ways.

You listen with a patient ear,

And I reach for you, knowing you'll be there,

Like the familiar scent of rain on pavement,

A constant, comforting presence.

We've woven ourselves into these routines,
But a life in the margins of calendar dates
And forgotten errands.
There's beauty in this rhythm,
In the way we navigate the mundane together,
Finding meaning in the ordinary,
Where love is not always spoken,
But felt in every glance, every touch.

When we lay down at night,
It's not the fireworks of first love,
But the quiet contentment of knowing we've crafted
Something lasting, something real.
And in the stillness,
I see us,
Perfectly imperfect,
In the simple harmony of what we've become.

WHERE WE ARE NOW

I know you feel it to-

How love changes shape over time.

We're no longer the wildfire we once were,

Burning so bright we couldn't see past the flame.

Now, It's different.

Your touch is a habit I never want to break,

Your voice is the background noise I can't live without.

It's not the heat of the sun anymore,

But the steady warmth of coals,

Burning slow, burning deep.

We've built this, quietly,

Through every argument we survived,

Through the nights we lay in silence,

Too tired to be anything but together.

And maybe we don't talk about it,

But I see it-

The way you stay.

Even when the days stretch long,

When the light fades early,

You're still here,

And that's enough.

HOW I LOVE YOU

I love you enough to stand in the storm,

To weather the rain and fight through the winds,

To shield you from darkness, to keep you from harm,

And carry the weight when your spirit thins.

Enough to reach out across any distance,

No matter how long the miles stretch between us.

Through endless nights or silent resistance,

With love as my compass, forever it frees us.

I love you in the quiet moments and the chaos,

When life pulls us apart or draws us near,

Holding your hand through the highs and the loss,

Believing in us when the path isn't clear.

I love you with a certainty that grows each day,

A devotion that deepens with time's steady flow,

Finding in you the reason I stay,

Cherishing every breath, every moment we know.

In your eyes,

I see all the lives we will live,

The dreams we will fulfil, the promises we keep.

I love you enough to give all I can give,

And still find more in the depths,

Where my love runs deep.

BEYOND WORDS

I loved you,

Long before language could find me,

Before words had meaning,

Before I knew what it was to name a feeling.

You were the quiet in my chest,

A pulse beneath my skin,

A rhythm I followed,

Without knowing why.

It's not in the things we say,

But in the silence between-

In the way you reach for me like it's instinct,

Where the heart speaks in whispers,

Only the soul can hear.

In the way your hand finds mine

In a room full of people,

Like it was always meant to be there.

Like the distance between us is something

You were born to close.

I love you in moments so small,

They could slip between seconds,

Like the brush of your hand against mine

When no one is watching,

Or the way your breath slows

When we share the same space.

There's a part of me that only exists in your eyes-

Like I become real the moment you look at me.

Like all the pieces I've scattered through my life

Find their way back,

When I'm with you.

I don't love you in grand gestures,

Or in words that try too hard.

I love you in the quiet unfolding of time,

In the way we fill spaces without even realising

We're building something that will outlast us.

It's the way we fit-

Not perfectly, but completely.

Like two jagged stones worn smooth by the same river,

Learning to rest side by side.

I loved you,

Before I even knew there was a word for love,

And I will love you,

Long after the words have gone.

A POEM FOR YOU

In the depths of my heart,

I feel a burning flame,

A passion that only you could ever claim.

My love for you is like a shining star,

Guiding me through life,

No matter where you are.

Your smile is like the sun,

Warming my soul,

Your laughter like music,

Making me feel whole.

No words can describe the way I feel,

A love so strong,

So pure, so real.

This poem is for you,

My heart and my soul,

A love that only you will ever know.

May it be a reminder of our love so true,

A love that only I can claim,

And only you.

A POET'S PEN

Beneath the canopy of a star-strewn sky,

Where the moon whispers secrets with a gentle sigh,

There dwells a poet, with pen in hand,

Casting verses like grains of sand.

With words that dance upon the page,

Ink flowing like a river's rage,

The poet's pen, a conduit of dreams,

A vessel for the soul's unseen streams.

It writes of love, of loss, of pain,

Of sunsets kissed by evening's rain,

It captures moments, fleeting and rare,

And etches them upon the air.

In the silence where whispers dwells,

It weaves a tale no tongue can tell.

It speaks of hearts both young and old,

Of stories hidden, yet to be told,

Of journeys taken through realms unseen,

Of battles fought and places serene.

In shadows deep, where secrets sleep,

It finds the thoughts we dare not keep,

It brings to light the hidden scars,

The dreams we've chased, the distant stars.

It captures echoes of the past,

The moments we hoped would always last,

And paints the future, broad and wide,

With strokes of courage, love, and pride.

In every line, a world unfolds,

Of mysteries and tales of old.

The poet's pen, with gentle grace,

Creates a time, a sacred space.

Where whispers turn to thunderous roars,

And silent dreams unlock their doors.

In every stroke, a soul is laid,

In every verse, a promise is made,

To tell the tales that hearts conceal,

To speak the truths that make us real.

ABOUT THE AUTHOR

Merisa Biscette is a Poet and Writer based in the United Kingdom. *A Poet's Pen* is her first poetry collection, exploring themes of love, loss, and self-discovery. Merisa Biscette draws inspiration from personal experiences and the world around, using poetry to give voice to the emotions we all feel but sometimes struggle to express.

Printed in Great Britain
by Amazon